Other Books by eXu Authors

Books by Dermot Davis and H Raven Rose

Mr. Psychic
Encounter

~

Books by Dermot Davis

Brain: The Man Who Wrote the Book That Changed the World
The Younger Man: How Many Times Can You Take a Second Chance on love?
Stormy Weather: A Novel: Are You Dreaming Now?
Fatal Eclipse
THE YOUNGER MAN: BOX SET (3 books in 1): How Many Times Can You Take Another Chance on love?
CAGED: A Short Reads Novella

~

Books by H Raven Rose

Dark Eros: a Novella
Shadow Selves (Double Happiness)
The Big "O": A Romantic Comedy
Dread Zone
Bugocalypse: la Cucaracha V1

~

Caffè Latte

Caffè Latte

5 VEGAN COFFEE DRINK RECIPES

VEGAN DIET

To the Reader

> *"THIS THINK BRINGED TO*
> *YOU BY MORE COFFEE!"*
>
> @FAKEGRIMLOCK

Introduction

WHAT IS CAFFÈ LATTE?

IF YOU DRINK coffee that you buy in a little coffee shop, then you have probably heard of caffè latte:[*]

CAFFÈ LATTE KĂF'Ā LÄ'TĀ, KÄF-FĔ' LÄT'TĔ

- n. A strong espresso coffee topped with steamed frothed miʟk.
- n. A serving of this beverage.
- n. strong espresso coffee with a topping of frothed steamed miʟk

Caffe ʟatte is a coffee drink made with espresso and steamed miʟk. The word comes from the Itaʟian caffè e ʟatte [kafˌfɛ e ʟ ˈʟatte], caffeʟatte [kaffeˈʟatte] or caffeʟʟatte [kaffeʟˈʟatte], which means "coffee & miʟk"(Latte, Wikipedia).

---

[*] caffe latte, Wordnik (*The American Heritage® Dictionary of the English Language*, 5th Edition): https://www.wordnik.com/words/caffe%20latte

Type: Hot and iced beverage, miLk coffee
PLace of origin: ItaLy
Main ingredients: espresso, steamed miLk

While it is really awesome to have a coffee or tea out while traveling in the world, on special occasions, or on dates out with friends or others, making your own hot coffee drinks is an affordable way to enjoy a delicious, whole foods, plant-based warming drink.

CRUELTY-FREE COFFEE IS COOL

While black coffee is naturally vegan, free from animal products, in the typical coffee shop, fancy coffee is not. While living a kind and cruelty-free life, you may miss creamy, decadent coffees with milk or whipped cream. The problem is that not only are these types of coffee drinks loaded with empty carbohydrates, but they are made with moo (and baby cows need that moo, not you).

This short book is here to rescue you from the boredom of same-old, same-old, at-home vegan coffee drinks made with nut, soy, oat, hemp, or other milk. Most recipes include stevia as the sweetener; however, feel free to use coconut sugar, maple, or rice syrup if carbs are not an issue for you and your gut health is fine.

Also, if you are hyper-nourishing in alignment with Dr. Goldner's Hyper-Nourishment program, sprouted hemp seeds make an outstanding Omega-3-rich vegan milk. Additionally, consider trying organic decaffeinated coffee or organic green or bancha twig (loose Japanese kukicha twig) tea as an occasional alternative, as excessive acid and caffeine can be harmful.

So, prop the print (or digital) version of this book up in your kitchen and refer to these recipes while you whip up a caffè latte or coffee. Know that what you're creating is ethical, kind to all life, and probably quite a bit more healthful than what you have given up. Enjoy your favorite coffee drinks vegan style.

The tools recommended in the recipes, including the Magical Bullet or other personal or high-speed blender, are expected to be found in most kitchens. Those items include a mug, coffee cup, or ceramic soup bowl with a handle, measuring utensils, a pot for warming ingredients, and the ingredients themselves.

Every recipe in this book is equally delicious, whether made with hot or cold green tea as an alternative to coffee. Additionally, you can switch most non-dairy milk to a different non-dairy milk option. For example, if you don't have unsweetened coconut, use almond or another nut or seed milk, soy or hemp, or oat milk.

If you don't have any non-dairy milk, you can make your own by combining fresh water with sprouted (soaked) nuts or seeds, such as almonds, hemp, or sunflower seeds, and blending them in a Magical Bullet or other blender. If you don't have seeds, use any nut butter on hand (blend and thin it with water). The choice of non-dairy milk, homemade or otherwise, will affect the flavor of the recipe.

It's fun to experiment with these recipes. Although I do not prefer dates for sweetening vegan foods or otherwise, many find that dates make an excellent sweetener. If you choose to use them, be sure to double-check that the pits have been removed. Then, soak the dates in hot or warm water before draining, as this helps them blend more easily.

Sometimes, I add a pinch or spoonful of organic turmeric powder to my hot drinks; it goes exceptionally well with cacao powder. Other organic powders that can enhance the deliciousness of these recipes include organic ground cinnamon, ginger, or nutmeg. However, I'm not a nutritionist or wellness expert, so please use these recipes at your own discretion.

This book came about because I wanted a vegan coffee recipe eBook (I like to put an e-reader on a stand in the kitchen while preparing vegan foods), and there wasn't one. So, I came up with and kitchen-tested a few quick vegan, easy, and delicious coffee drink recipes, and then a book was drafted post-haste. By the way, the Caffè Latte print book version has black and white photographs. To view the beautiful, colored images, please purchase the ebook.

Thank you for reading. Negative reviews can be particularly damaging to authors, so please don't hesitate to contact us if you have suggestions on how we might improve the work.

Please let me know of suggestions for this ebook or errors via:

https://hravenroseauthor.com/contact

To your good health!

H Raven Rose

PS. Perhaps you're not vegan, but please know that there are many benefits to adopting this lifestyle. From healthline.com, "6 Science-Based Health Benefits of Eating Vegan," written by Alina Petre, MS, RD, LDN, on September 23, 2016:[*]

---

[*] *6 Science-Based Health Benefits of Eating Vegan*: https://www.healthline.com/nutrition/vegan-diet-benefits

- Vegan diets often help people trim down.
- Additionally, vegan diets offer health benefits.
- A vegan diet may keep your heart healthier.
- Plus, vegan foods may reduce the chance of illness.

- Vegan diets often help people trim down.
- Additionally, vegan diets offer health benefits.
- A vegan diet may keep your heart healthier.
- Plus, vegan foods may reduce the chance of illness.

Pink Love You a Latte
VEGAN BEETROOT LATTE

Photo by **ROMAN ODINTSOV** *from* **Pexels**

OH, IT IS PINK. OH, IT IS PRETTY. A deep pink or
nearly red LATTe is a Valentine for your mouth. Beets are not
just a pretty face. Beetroot is rich in fiber and contains a variety

of vitamins, including folate, manganese, magnesium, and potassium. A single serving of beetroot has 4% of the recommended daily intake of iron, as well as plant compounds that are good for you.

INGREDIENTS US, 1 SERVING

- 1-2 organic beetroot (smallish, raw)
- 1 cup unsweetened almond milk (or another nut or seed milk), organic if possible
- 1/4 teaspoon organic cinnamon powder, 1 pinch organic nutmeg
- 1 pinch organic ginger powder
- 1/2 to 1 teaspoon cold-pressed organic coconut oil (raw pressed)
- 1/8 cup brewed espresso or strongly brewed coffee, organic if possible
- Stevia to taste

HOW TO PREPARE this **cup of love, aka Pink Love You a Latte (Vegan Beetroot Latte)**:

1. Wash the beetroot well, then peel and chop it into very small pieces.
2. Put all the ingredients except nut milk and stevia into a Magical Bullet or other personal blender.
3. Add 1/4 cup warm pure water to the blender. Blend ingredients until fine, usually a minute or two.
4. Heat the nut milk till it simmers (don't let it boil).
5. Add the nut milk to the blender and blend it carefully and quickly. (*Be careful with this step as a "too hot" liquid will usually leak and spurt from the Magical Bullet.*)
6. Add fresh-brewed organic espresso or strongly brewed coffee (just enough to flavor it), and some stevia to suit your taste.

Pour into a beautiful cup and serve yourself up some pink liquid love. Enjoy!

Moo-free Caffè Latte

CLASSIC COFFEE + VEGAN CREAM

*Photo by **Delphine Hourlay** from **Pexels***

THERE IS no doubt that the caffeine in coffee or espresso can be a nice little kick in the seat of your productivity pants.

However, almost every caffè latte purchased at a local café or coffee shop is heavy on the milk. You could ask for dairy-free milk alternatives, including drinks made with nuts or seeds, soy, oats, or even hemp.

However, most of the time, the coffee shop's milk alternatives are not unsweetened, and these alternatives usually contain preservatives and other additives. Plus, why go out and pay $5 a pop to cuddle up with a cuppa? Get the creamy coffee comfort with this quick and easy, delicious vegan hot drink.

INGREDIENTS US, 1 SERVING

- 1/2 to 1 TBL raw almond or cashew butter, 1/2 to 1 teaspoon cold-pressed organic coconut oil (raw pressed)
- 1-2 cups brewed espresso or strongly brewed coffee, organic if possible
- Stevia to taste (or blend in 1-2 pitted organic Medjool dates if you have a serious sweet tooth)

HOW TO PREPARE this **cup of cruelty-free deliciousness (Moo-Free Caffè Latte)**:

1. Combine the ingredients, including the Medjool dates (if using those), in your Magical Bullet or other high-speed blender. Blend the ingredients until smooth and frothy. (Be careful with this step as too hot liquid will usually leak and spurt from the Magical Bullet.)
2. If your coffee is cold or cool, you can warm the blended mixture in a pan on the stove.
3. Lastly, pour your coffee mixture into a beautiful cup and add stevia, as desired, to suit your taste. Enjoy!

NOTE: You can try the chillax summer version of this recipe by using cool or cold-brewed coffee in the blend and then serving the mixture over ice in a glass or mason jar.

Pumpkin Spice Latte

COZY CUP OF AUTUMN SPICEY-SWEET

*Photo by **Valeriia Miller** from **Pexels***

IS AUTUMN THE START OF THE BEST SEASON FOR HOT COFFEE DRINKS? The snap of a crisp, cool fall day, a walk to look at colorful fall leaves, and a warm mug or cup of pumpkin spice latte go hand in hand. Although this recipe takes a bit of time to prepare, it's a pumpkin pie drink that melts in your mouth, making it worth it.

INGREDIENTS US, 1-2 SERVINGS

- 1/3 cup organic pumpkin purée
- 1 cup of unsweetened almond milk (or another nut or seed milk), organic if possible
- 1/8 teaspoon organic pure vanilla bean extract, 1 pinch organic pumpkin pie spice
- 1/2 to 1 teaspoon cold-pressed organic coconut oil (raw pressed)
- 1 cup brewed espresso or strongly brewed coffee, organic if possible (use more or less according to preference)
- stevia to taste

HOW TO PREPARE **this pumpkin pie in a cup (Pumpkin Spice latte)**

1. Add unsweetened nut milk to a saucepan and use a spatula to gently stir in the organic pumpkin purée, the organic pure vanilla extract, and the pumpkin pie spice. Heat the ingredients until they gently simmer (*do not let them boil, just heat until quite warm*).
2. Remove your pan from the heat. Pour the mixture into a tall coffee mug or evenly distribute it between two coffee mugs. Top up the mug with organic espresso or strongly brewed coffee and stir in.
3. Add a sweetener; stevia is generally suggested, according to your personal preference and health requirements. Stir in the cold-pressed organic coconut oil (it makes the latte SO creamy delicious).

4. Top your latte with vegan whipped cream or frothed nut milk *. Then add a sprinkle of organic pumpkin pie spice.

5. For a bit of extra presentation flair, add a sprig of organic rosemary to this concoction. Enjoy!

NOTE: You can create a simple homemade pumpkin pie spice by combining equal amounts of ground cinnamon, ground ginger, ground nutmeg, ground allspice, and ground cloves (ideally organic).

*The Magical Bullet is aces at blending soaked or sprouted hemp seeds, or nuts, and pure water into a frothy nut milk.

HOT CHOCOLATEY COFFEE

*Photo by **Victor Freitas** from **Pexels***

OH, IT IS DARK, IT IS SWEET, DARK, AND OH-SO-DELICIOUS!

A caffè mocha, or mochaccino, also called a mocha latte, is a rich love letter for your body, mind, and spirit. Antioxidant-rich raw cacao powder is a natural stimulant due to theobromine. Chocolate offers numerous benefits, including antioxidants such as flavanols and procyanidins, which provide cellular defense against damaging free radicals.

Each serving of antioxidants may help improve the look of skin by promoting cellular rejuvenation and repair. The raw and organic cold-processed cacao makes a superior hot mocha; careful processing retains the nutritional benefits. Plus, is there anything better with coffee than chocolate?

INGREDIENTS US, 1 SERVING

- 1 cup unsweetened coconut or almond, or other nut, seed, soy, hemp, or oat milk, organic if possible
- 2 TBL raw organic cacao powder
- 1/4 teaspoon organic vanilla bean extract
- 1/2 to 1 teaspoon cold-pressed organic coconut oil (raw pressed)
- 1 cup brewed espresso or strongly brewed coffee, organic if possible
- Stevia to taste (or 1-2 Medjool dates)

HOW TO PREPARE this cup of dark love, aka Mocha (Hot Chocolatey Coffee)

1. Combine the ingredients, including the Medjool dates (if using), in your Magical Bullet or other high-speed blender. Blend the ingredients until smooth and frothy. (Be careful with this step as too hot liquid will usually leak and spurt from the Magical Bullet.)

2. If your mocha is cold or cool, slightly warm the blended mixture in a pan on the stove.
3. Lastly, pour your coffee mixture into a beautiful cup or mug and add stevia, as desired or needed, to suit your taste. Enjoy!

NOTE: Stirring your Mocha with a sugar-free, organic peppermint stick is a fun nod to the winter holidays. Alternatively, try the chillax summer version of this recipe by using cool or cold-brewed coffee in the blender, then serving the mixture over ice in a glass or mason jar without heating it.

Moo-free Matcha Latte

IT'S EASY BEING GREEN

Photo by **Charlotte May** from **Pexels**

TAKE A WALK ON THE GREEN SIDE, MY FRIEND, AND TRY making this easy vegan matcha latte at home! This yummy recipe is quick, vegan, and requires just a few ingredients.

Matcha contains antioxidants, numerous nutrients (including vitamin C, selenium, zinc, magnesium, and more), is believed to be immune-boosting, and features L-Theanine. The L-theanine, combined with the caffeine in matcha, leads to an experience of sustained, focused energy and may support a state of flow.

Some say that matcha will help you detoxify, boost your metabolism, and also calm your mind. The best matcha is organic, finely ground, additive-free, of ceremonial quality, and of Japanese origin. Matcha powder can be a bit spendy for some, yet you only need a small amount to make a drink.

*Photo by **Delphine Hourlay** from **Pexels***

MATCHA IS GRADED from lowest to highest quality based upon the color, texture, aroma, flavor, and freshness. Culinary-grade matcha is available, but ceremonial-grade matcha is the highest quality and is recommended for drinking. Please note that ceremonial-grade matcha, sourced from respected farms in Japan, is traditionally not prepared with additives (such as the nut milk and sweeteners commonly used in the West).

Choosing great matcha depends on what is available in your area (or online, if you have access) and the type you select. The brighter the green, the better the matcha, or so it is said.

Additionally, please note that, unlike our intention here, the ceremonial use and preparation of matcha are somewhat complex and require specialized tools and techniques.

A traditional Japanese matcha ceremony typically involves a Chawan (a ceramic matcha tea bowl with a depth adjusted according to the season) and a bamboo whisk known as a chasen. There are other tools, including a special tool for scooping matcha, sifters, and more.

So, for our non-ceremonial at-home vegan hot drink purposes, you only need a way to blend, heat, and measure your ingredients.

INGREDIENTS US, 1 SERVING

- 1 cup unsweetened almond milk (or non-dairy milk of choice)
- 1 to 1 1/2 teaspoons ceremonial grade matcha powder (or to taste)
- Stevia, to taste, or 1 or 2 pitted Medjool dates

HOW TO PREPARE **THIS DETOX IN A CUP (Moo-Free Matcha latte)**

1. Warm your organic nut, seed, soy, hemp, or other milk until it simmers (don't let it boil).
2. Combine the non-dairy milk, matcha, and the Medjool dates (if using) in your Magical Bullet or other high-speed blender. Blend the ingredients until smooth and frothy. (Be careful with this step as too hot liquid will usually leak and spurt from the Magical Bullet.)
3. Lastly, pour your matcha mixture into a beautiful soup bowl with a handle or oversized mug and add stevia, as desired or needed (unless you used dates to sweeten), to suit your taste. Enjoy!

NOTE: You can try the chillax summer version of this recipe by making the matcha and then letting it cool. When it is cool enough, serve the mixture over ice.

Thank you for reading this book. Remember to love yourself and warm your hands and heart by sipping on healthful, nurturing, and delish vegan drinks.

About the Editor

In between drinking vegan caffè lattes, award-winning filmmaker, screenwriter, and author, H Raven Rose, bleeds stardust-tinted ink and writes story worlds from beyond the stars. Her MFA and PhD are in creative writing, and she is an award-winning screenwriter/director, author, poet, playwright, and creativity researcher; her poem painted in film—*Sacred Birthday, Sacred Wales - Pen-Blwydd yn Gysegredig, Cymru Sanctaidd*—won the 2021 Wales International Film Festival Illustrated Poem Jury's Award Special Prize. In 2018, her short live-action film *Sleep Disturbance* was shot on Super 8 film in Bristol and screened at The Cube Microplex, Bristol, UK. Her play *Dark Eros*, adapted into a suspense novella of the same title, was staged as readings in Los Angeles, with one production starring Jessica Biel in the lead role as Leila. An excerpt of the play version of *Sleep Disturbance* was staged as readings at the Taliesin Create Space. Recent publications include creative nonfiction, 'Waking up Wild' and 'Snow', published in *Tofu Ink Arts Press*, the ecopoem '23 Species from 19 States lost to extinction' published in the Winter 2022 edition of *In Parentheses*, and 'Mars or Bust: How Science Fiction Films will Promote Mars Colonization Reality' published in the newly released *The Book of Mars: An Anthology of Fact and Fiction* edited by Dr Stuart Clark (presented initially at The Mars Society 21st Annual International Convention in 2018 in Pasadena, CA). A member of the

Screenwriting Research Network and Women in Film LA, her practice-led creativity research explores writing flow, writer's blocks, and creativity within the framework of childhood development following developmental trauma. Follow H on Goodreads or Substack @hravenrose.

Find H online at:
https://hravenroseauthor.com/
https://hravenrose.substack.com/
https://www.goodreads.com/hravenrose/

goodreads.com/hravenrose

pinterest.com/hravenrose

bookbub.com/authors/h-raven-rose

Newsletter

If you liked this book, please leave a positive review of it online (and recommend it)!

Love to read?! Sign up for eXu Publishing news to learn about new fiction releases by H Raven Rose, Dermot Davis, and other authors: https://www.exupublishing.com/

Love sci-fi? Sign up for H Raven Rose's newsletter for information on new speculative fiction or other book or film releases: https://hravenroseauthor.com/